THE PIRATE KING

TORNO
THE
HURRICANE
DRAGON

With special thanks to Cherith Baldry

To Elliot

www.beastquest.co.uk

ORCHARD BOOKS
338 Euston Road, London NW1 3BH
Orchard Books Australia
Level 17/207 Kent St, Sydney, NSW 2000

A Paperback Original
First published in Great Britain in 2011

Beast Quest is a registered trademark of Beast Quest Limited
Series created by Working Partners Limited, London

Text © Beast Quest Limited 2011
Inside illustrations by Pulsar Estudio (Beehive Illustration)
Cover illustrations by Steve Sims © Orchard Books 2011

A CIP catalogue record for this book is available from
the British Library.

ISBN 978 1 40831 313 8

Printed and bound in China by Imago

The paper and board used in this paperback are natural recyclable
products made from wood grown in sustainable forests. The
manufacturing processes conform to the environmental regulations of
the country of origin.

Orchard Books is a division of Hachette Children's Books,
an Hachette UK company

www.hachette.co.uk

TornO
THE
HURRICANE
DRAGON

BY ADAM BLADE

ORCHARD BOOKS

Tremble, warriors of Avantia, for a new enemy stalks your land!

I am Sanpao, the Pirate King of Makai! My ship brings me to your shores to claim an ancient magic more powerful than any you've encountered before. No one can stand in my way, especially not that pathetic boy, Tom, or his friends. Even Aduro cannot help you this time. My pirate band will pillage and burn without mercy, and my Beasts will be more than a match for any hero in Avantia.

Pirates! Batten down the hatches and raise the sails. We come to conquer and destroy!

Sanpao, the Pirate King

PROLOGUE

"Go, Redwind!"

Hal smiled as his beloved falcon spread its wings and mounted high into the air, the bells on its legs tinkling. The sight of the magnificent bird soaring over Avantia's northern mountains had gladdened Hal's heart for years.

Redwing was on majestic form today. Hal had to narrow his eyes against the sunlight to pick out the shape of the falcon swooping in and out of the rocky mountain peaks.

"You're the finest bird in all Avantia," he said. "And you're going to win the annual Northern Avantia Wing Race – I just know—"

Hal broke off. Redwind had paused in mid-flight. At first Hal thought the falcon had spotted some prey on the mountain slopes, and was preparing to swoop. But Redwind's wings were spread wide, like he was soaring. And yet, he didn't make the slightest movement. It was like he wasn't a real bird at all, but a painting on the sky.

Hal raised his arm, in the signal for his falcon to fly down to him. "Redwind, here!"

But Redwind didn't move.

What's going on? Hal asked himself anxiously.

He was about to call again when

a fierce gust of wind came out of
nowhere, snatching his breath away.
The gust knocked him to his knees.

Hal struggled against the force of
the gale, which felt like a giant hand
pinning him to the ground. Finally,
he managed to get to his feet, looking
up to see Redwind beating his wings.
Now Hal understood: the magnificent

bird was trying to fly against the freak wind, but he couldn't make any progress.

As he fought to stand upright, Hal glimpsed a shimmer of gold gleaming from behind one of the rocky mountain tops. An enormous, lizard-like head appeared just below the struggling falcon, its scales dazzling in the sunlight and its wide jaws gaping open.

The gust of wind seems to be coming from its mouth, Hal realised. *Oh no – Redwind!*

Hal tried calling out a warning to his falcon, but the wind swallowed his voice again. He could do nothing but stare in horror as the Beast's jaws snapped shut over his winged friend.

Instantly the hurricane disappeared as if a giant door had been slammed against it. Hal dropped to his knees. "No!"

Through his tears of distress, Hal looked up and saw the full form of the terrible Beast as it emerged from behind the rocks. Trailing back from the lizard head was a long dragon's body covered in shining golden scales and a row of spikes running along its spine. A pair of wings jutted from its sleek, muscled body, sweeping strongly down as the creature leaped into the air to hover over the topmost peak.

Its claws glittered like diamonds and dug deep into the rock as the Beast alighted on a mountain ledge. Perched on the stony peak, the monster let out a snort of triumph and angled its head downwards.

Hal backed away, sensing the

Beast's eyes fixed on him, then turned and ran. Glancing over his shoulder, he saw the Beast taking to the air, its mighty talons ripping great gouges in the mountain as it swooped. Hal caught the foul reek of its breath and heard the swish of its wings cutting the air. His feet pounded the rough moorland grass, which was so long he couldn't see the jutting stone that tripped him up. He crashed headlong to the ground. Everything went dark as the Beast's shadow fell over him.

CHAPTER ONE

THE ROAD NORTH

Tom tugged on Storm's reins,
drawing his black stallion to a halt,
and pulled out the tree-bark map
from his saddlebag. He and Elenna
had reached the very edge of
Avantia's Central Plains, and the
Northern Mountains reared up
ahead, their forbidding rocky peaks
outlined against the sky.

Tom unrolled the map and peered

at the outlines of Avantia's roads, rivers and hills, then shook his head. "The Tree of Being still hasn't appeared," he told Elenna.

Elenna manoeuvred closer on her white mare, Blizzard, so that she could lean over and look at the map.

"It's never taken this long before," she said. "We need *something* to tell us where to find it. Otherwise…"

Elenna didn't finish her thought. She didn't need to.

Tom rolled up the map and put it away, trying not to think about what would happen if Sanpao and his pirates caught up with them. He and Elenna needed to get to the Tree of Being first.

Tom pulled his golden compass out of his saddlebag. "The needle is still pointing towards Destiny," he said.

"We should press on northwards."

"If the Tree of Being reappears in the south or west," Elenna murmured anxiously, "we're in big trouble. What if it's wrong?"

"The compass has never steered us wrong before," said Tom. Stowing away the compass, he urged Storm into a trot. As they moved on, Tom glanced over his shoulder to see that the last traces of the forest had disappeared behind them. He and Elenna were tired from their battle with Hecton the Body Snatcher, but Tom knew that they couldn't rest yet. Avantia was still under the gravest threat it had ever known.

"We *have* to get to the Tree first," Tom muttered to himself. "If Sanpao the Pirate King gets his hands on it, he'll be able to use its powers to raid any other land he likes."

But that wasn't the only reason why Tom's stomach churned at the thought of losing the race with the pirates. The Tree of Being would also open up a portal to Tavania, where Tom's mother, Freya, and Elenna's pet wolf, Silver, had been left stranded at the end of their last Beast Quest.

Getting to the Tree first is our only chance of rescuing them, Tom thought grimly. "Sanpao may be clever," he said, "but we can out-think him, and we've got the best reason in the world not to give up." He touched the trident that he had won in his combat against Hecton; he had cut off the shaft so that it would fit into his sash. "We have the weapons we need, too. Nothing can stop us!"

As he finished speaking, a fork of

blue lightning crackled down from the sky. Storm reared, striking at the air with his hooves. Tom had to grip tightly with his knees to stop himself being thrown from the saddle. Blizzard let out a high-pitched whinny and stepped sideways, her hooves slipping on the stones. Elenna leaned forward, patting the nervous mare's neck soothingly.

Tom was still tugging hard on Storm's reins when the crack of lightning expanded into a shimmering blue globe, with the figure of Wizard Aduro inside it. His form was faint; Tom could still see the outline of the mountains through it.

"Aduro!" Tom glanced at Elenna. "Do you think Sanpao has sent him?" he asked her quietly.

"I don't know." Elenna's voice was

sharp with suspicion. "But we shouldn't trust him."

Before Tom and Elenna set out, Sanpao had put the Good Wizard under an evil spell. During the last stage of their Quest, Aduro had managed to send a faint message to Tom that showed he was fighting

with all his strength against the dark magic. Tom hoped that Aduro was sending another message now, to prove that Sanpao's hold on him was beginning to weaken.

Tom's hope died as he saw the cold sneer on Aduro's face and the malicious glimmer in his eyes.

"Why don't you just turn back?" the Wizard asked, his voice an unrecognisable snarl. "What hope do you have of taking on so many pirates?"

"We've vanquished tougher enemies than Sanpao," Tom told him, trying to sound strong.

"It takes more than cutlasses to frighten us," Elenna added.

Aduro snorted in contempt. "Your luck is soon going to run out."

For a moment Tom couldn't find the words to reply. Aduro had never sounded as hostile as this, even when he first fell victim to Sanpao's magic.

"I hope the real Aduro can hear me," he began, keeping his voice calm. "Don't worry – while there's blood in my veins, I shan't rest until you're set free."

Aduro let out a wordless growl and vanished, leaving behind a wisp of blue light that quickly faded.

"Strange," Elenna said, a faint frown furrowing her brows. "All Aduro did was to spout a few empty threats. What was it all about?"

Tom shrugged. "Sanpao is up to something. I'm going to check the map again."

He delved into his saddlebag and produced the thin bark scroll. A rush of relief filled him as he looked it over. "Now I understand!" he exclaimed, pointing at the map.

With Elenna leaning over to look at the outline traced on the bark, Tom studied the tiny picture of the Tree of Being that had finally returned, sprouting among the topmost peaks of the Northern Mountains.

"Sanpao can't land his ship among all the rocks and outcrops, can he?" he asked, feeling a grin spread over his face. "He knows we'll beat him to the Tree, so he sent Aduro to scare us off."

"Well, it didn't work!" Elenna said.

Tom dug his heels into Storm's side, spurring the stallion into a gallop. Elenna and Blizzard raced along at his shoulder. As the wind blew through his hair, Tom felt a surge of new energy. *Maybe this Beast Quest is turning in our favour at last!*

CHAPTER TWO

TRAPS!

The first stars were beginning to
appear by the time Tom and Elenna
reached the foothills of the Northern
Mountains. In the distance, Tom
could just make out the rooftops of
the town of Colton, with thin plumes
of smoke rising lazily into the
evening air.

Using the map, Tom found
a narrow path that led through the

foothills and snaked up into the mountains, heading towards the place on the map where the Tree of Being was marked. Elenna took the lead as their horses picked their way carefully among the loose stones.

As they climbed higher, the path grew steeper, and a sheer drop opened up on one side. In the shadows below, Tom made out sharp rocks, and heard the faint gurgle of a stream.

Tom kept looking up at the sky, alert for any sign of the flying pirate ship. He expected to see the vessel's threatening outline, and to hear the crack of sails, the creaking of timbers and Sanpao's voice shouting orders to his crew. But nothing disturbed the thin cloud that stretched across the darkening sky.

I mustn't get too confident, he thought. *Sanpao is cunning. He's bound to be making some sort of plan.*

He was trying to think what the Pirate King's plot could be, when suddenly Elenna let out a cry of alarm. Blizzard reared up, coming perilously close to the edge of the cliff. Elenna clung to the saddle and steered the mare to safety.

Spooked by Blizzard's sudden movement, Storm reared too, one flying hoof striking sparks from a jutting rock as he leaped aside. Tom leaned forward, stroking his neck. "Steady, boy. Steady."

To his relief, Storm quickly grew calm again, and Elenna managed to regain control of Blizzard. The mare stood still, sweat breaking out on her glossy white neck.

"What happened?" Tom asked, trying to peer past Elenna to see what was up ahead.

"She's spotted something on the track," Elenna explained. "Look!"

Guiding Storm up closer to Blizzard, Tom made out a long stretch of rusty iron jaws along the next section of the path. They were nearly invisible in the gathering darkness.

"Animal traps!" Tom said, reaching across to pat the mare's neck. "Well done, Blizzard."

He dismounted to look closer at the traps and investigate. Vicious teeth lined the metal springs.

"They're fastened with a chain and a bolt driven into the rock face," Tom called back to Elenna. "We'll never be able to move them."

Tom broke off a branch from a

scrawny bush that had rooted itself in a crack, and used it to prod the nearest trap. The jaws snapped shut with a loud crack, smashing the branch to splinters. Tom shuddered: *That could have been Storm or Blizzard's legs!*

"The horses will never manage to pick their way through," he said to Elenna as he returned to Storm and climbed into the saddle. "We'll have to find another route around."

Elenna nodded. "By the time we've done that, it will be almost night," she said. "Far too dark for us to be walking around in terrain this dangerous."

Tom gripped Storm's reins in anger. "Sanpao isn't stupid!" he burst out. "He must have sent some scouts ahead to lay these traps here, to delay us while he works out how to land his ship among the rocky peaks."

"Which means there might be pirates around here," Elenna pointed out as they began cautiously making their way back down the path.

"I know," Tom replied, glancing back. "We'll find somewhere to shelter here in the mountains and set off again at dawn."

"What about the pirates?" asked Elenna. "How can we sleep when there's a scouting party lurking in the shadows?"

Tom knew that his friend spoke sense. He frowned as he guided Storm down the path, then felt a smile grow slowly on his face.

"I have an idea," he said.

"Oh?" Elenna's face brightened with interest. "What are we going to do?"

"Wait and see," Tom replied. "I'll need a bit of parchment to draw a map, and your hunting knife..."

CHAPTER THREE

TOM'S PLAN

Tom shivered as he propped up his
shield at the entrance of the cave
where he and Elenna had taken
shelter for the night. A thin layer of
frost had formed on the rocks outside,
but the bell from Nanook the Snow
Monster kept away much of the
night-time cold. Elenna was crouched
over a small heap of kindling, blowing
on it to get a fire started.

In the darkness at the back of the cave Tom could just make out the shapes of Storm and Blizzard. Now and again, he heard their snuffling breath, and the scrape of a hoof on the ground.

Elenna built up the fire with thicker chunks of wood and began laying out their blankets beside it. "The pirates won't be able to miss that," she remarked, gazing up at the thin plume of smoke that curled up into the night air.

"You're right," Tom said with satisfaction. "So we'd better be ready for them."

Taking Elenna's hunting knife, he scrawled an 'X' on the map of the mountains he had copied from the tree bark, and laid it carefully on the floor inside the circle of firelight.

Then he rolled himself in his blanket and lay down, keeping his eyes open a crack so that he could watch.

Elenna did the same. Tom could hear her shifting and wriggling around to get comfortable. A moment later she let out a loud, fake snore.

Elenna's really getting into the spirit of this! Tom would have laughed if the situation wasn't so deadly. If his plan didn't work, they could be captured or killed by Sanpao's pirates. Under cover of the blanket, Tom gripped the hilt of his sword, ready to fight if he had to.

Sooner than he had expected, Tom heard footsteps approaching up the path and halting at the mouth of the cave.

Sanpao's pirate scouts had arrived. *Three of them*, Tom guessed. A moment later he heard the scrape of metal as three cutlasses were drawn.

One of the pirates let out a low cackle of laughter. "Look at 'em!" he whispered. "They're not even keeping watch."

"All to the good," a second voice answered. "Let's get the job done."

"Sanpao should pay us well for this," a third voice added.

A jolt of fear hit Tom in the stomach and he felt his heartbeat quicken. *They haven't seen the map!*

Footsteps shuffled forward, then stopped. "Hold up!" the first pirate said. "What's that?"

"It's nothing," the second man replied. "Just a rolled-up bit of parchment."

Tension crawled through Tom. With his eyes open a crack, he peered

towards the entrance of the cave and
saw three pirates standing there, lit by
the red glow of the fire. All three of
them were tall and muscular, wearing
sleeveless leather jerkins and loose
trousers tucked into boots. The tallest
of the three was close enough for
Tom to make out Sanpao's mark of
a Beast's skull on his brawny forearm.

Tom felt his heart race as the pirate nudged the parchment map with his boot. *Go on, pick it up,* he thought.

"We should take a look," another pirate argued, his thin, rat-like face alive with greed. He stooped and snatched up the scrap of parchment, letting out a gasp as he unrolled it. "It's a map!"

"And look at that 'X' in the mountains," the third pirate added, jabbing at the map with a stubby finger. "What do you think it means?"

Tom gritted his teeth to keep his breathing under control as he listened to the pirates muttering, their heads close together over the map he had drawn.

"It must be a treasure map," said one. "It's telling us there's something hidden in the mountains."

"What sort of treasure?" asked the rat-faced one.

"Gold? Silver? Maybe diamonds!"

"Who cares?" The voice of the tallest pirate rose above the others. "There's no such thing as bad hidden treasure. Let's go!"

"No – wait," the second pirate protested. "Sanpao won't be happy if we ignore his orders."

The tallest pirate let out a loud snort. "Sanpao won't care when he gets his share of the loot. Besides, we can come back later to deal with these so-called Avantian *heroes*. They're only children!"

A wave of relief washed over Tom as the pirates sheathed their blades. They turned and crept out of the cave, footsteps quickly fading away. When everything was quiet again he sat up and let out a long sigh.

"I can't believe they fell for it," he commented.

"Stupid pirates!" hissed Elenna, her eyes shining.

With Elenna beside him, Tom crawled to the cave entrance. The pirates' voices floated up faintly from somewhere below:

"It's this way – past that rock."

"I hope this path doesn't get any steeper."

"Stop moaning, you dolt. We'll be rich!"

"They *are* stupid," Tom said. "They think they're going to find some loot. But you know where they're *really* going, don't you?"

Elenna nodded, her eyes gleaming. "They're going to wake up Avantia's sleeping Mountain Giant!"

"Yes," said Tom. "The cross I marked on the map shows the Place of Eagles, where Arcta's lair is."

Elenna stifled laughter with a hand over her mouth. "That's so clever! Arcta will make them really welcome."

"And they won't bother *us* again," Tom added with satisfaction.

CHAPTER FOUR

WIND IN THE MOUNTAINS

Tom rubbed Storm's nose. "You and Blizzard will have to stay here in the cave," he said. "The paths are too steep for you to go any further."

"We'll come back for you soon," Elenna added, ruffling Blizzard's white mane.

Leaving the horses at the back of the cave, Tom and Elenna ventured out on to the path. It was still early in the morning, and shadows covered the mountains. Tom pulled out the tree-bark map and checked it quickly, then pointed up the path.

"This way," he said.

The twisting path snaked up the mountainside; Tom felt an icy trickle of fear between his shoulder blades at the thought that the jutting boulders could be hiding an enemy.

"Anything could be creeping up on us, and we'd never know it. And the path is so narrow. Keep to the inner edge," he advised Elenna, "and use the rock wall as a guide."

As he heaved himself up a deep shelf in the rock, Tom's foot skidded, scattering a small bundle of broken bones.

"What's that?" Elenna asked,

crouching down beside the remains.

Tom stooped beside her. "I think it was a bird," he said.

Elenna shivered. "Looks like it was once a falcon."

The sun came up over the mountain peaks. As they climbed higher, Tom found that he could see more clearly where they were going; endless peaks stretched in front of them, separated by steep, stony valleys.

Tom heard a deep, rumbling roar in the distance. It was followed by shouts and screams of terror.

He grinned at Elenna. "I think the pirates have met Arcta."

Elenna laughed. "That will teach them!"

Tom nodded. "Now there's nothing to stop us finding the Tree of Being."

The path grew steeper; Tom's legs

ached as he struggled upwards. His
feet kept slipping on the loose stones.

"It would be easier to climb. Can
you manage that?" he asked Elenna,
gazing towards the top of the sheer
cliff that rose alongside the path.

Elenna nodded vigorously. "Lead
the way!"

Tom went ahead, glancing down to

make sure that Elenna was following safely. He had to force his fingers and toes into cracks to edge his way up. But about half-way to the top of the cliff, the precipice levelled off a little, and the cliff face was filled with deep holes the perfect size for hands and feet.

"This is better than I'd hoped!" said Tom.

Tom found a swift rhythm and the top of the cliff grew closer. But as he reached for a jutting rock about halfway up, a sudden gust of wind almost tore him from the cliff face.

"Hold on tight!" he yelled to Elenna, digging his fingers and toes into cracks.

He glanced down to see Elenna clinging to the rocks as the wind buffeted her.

"This is strange," she called. "The wind is warm! Shouldn't it be cold, if we're this high up?"

Tom realised that his friend was right. This high in the mountains they ought to meet freezing gales, but this wind was as warm as a summer breeze – and far stronger. Looking around, he couldn't see anything that might be causing it.

Tom shook his head clear. The wind was the least of his problems just now. He needed to concentrate on the climb.

"We need to get off this cliff," he called to Elenna.

Glancing down at his friend again, he saw that she wasn't looking up at him. She was staring off to the left, her eyes wide with disbelief.

"What's wrong?" Tom asked.

"Can't you see?" Elenna replied. "These aren't natural handholds. They're claw prints!"

Tom's chest tightened as he looked for himself. Elenna was right! The crevices were in the shape of gigantic claws, rough circles with four deep channels splaying out from them. It looked as if some huge creature had sunk its feet deep into the mountain.

Tom gulped. *Is this the first sign of the Beast?*

A golden glare flashed out from the mountain peak above. His eyes instinctively snapped shut against the dazzling light that filled his vision.

Squinting, Tom peered at the mountain slope; a wide expanse of tumbled boulders separated it from where he clung to the cliff. Then, as his eyes grew used to the light, he made out the terrifying shape of a dragon! Sunlight reflected off its shining, golden scales, and its claws glittered like deadly jewels. Leathery wings stretched above its back, and the jaws of its vast lizard-like head were gaping as it let out a rumbling roar.

From below, Tom heard a cry from Elenna as she spotted the hideous Beast. "That's where the wind is coming from!" she yelled.

Tom's gaze was fixed on the golden dragon's size and threatening posture. At first, he didn't notice what the Beast was perching on, but then he started to take in the shape of twisted roots clinging to the mountainside, and branches jutting out into the air.

"Elenna," he said hoarsely. "That's the Tree of Being!"

CHAPTER FIVE

THE TREE OF BEING

The Beast's eyes flashed as it lifted its
head with another bellow. The Tree
of Being had sprouted out of the
mountainside at an angle. Its roots
gripped the mountain face like
gnarled fingers. Tom thought the Tree
looked stronger and healthier than
before; its branches were sturdier,
and its green leaves had a glossy

sheen. He couldn't see how the roots managed to support its weight among the rocks.

"It could crash down at any time," Tom said to Elenna. "We've got to hurry. Once we reach the Tree, we can go through the portal to Tavania and rescue Freya and Silver. We can finish this Beast Quest right now!"

"But we can't reach the Tree with that dragon perching on it," Elenna pointed out.

"It won't be perching there for long!" Tom replied confidently.

With Elenna close behind him, he climbed higher and faster, scrambling diagonally across the face of the cliff. He chose a route that brought him on to a wide ledge a little way above the Beast.

All the while he climbed, Tom

scarcely took his eyes off the dragon. Its head turned towards him, but it made no move to attack.

"Why isn't it moving?" Elenna panted, hauling herself on to the ledge beside him.

"I don't know," said Tom. The Beast's gaze was fixed on them. Its scales shone brighter still in the growing sunlight and its eyes gleamed with menace. But it did not move.

"What are we going to do?" Elenna asked.

Tom swung his shield down from his back and drew his sword. "I'm going to play the Beast's game," he replied, striding forward and halting just above the Beast. Tom thought he could see a teasing glint in the dragon's eyes.

"Don't challenge me," he muttered aloud. "You'll regret it."

Tom held his shield above his head, focusing on the power of Arcta's eagle feather set into its surface.

Elenna was clambering after him. "Be careful!" she called.

"For Avantia!" Tom cried, and leaped off the ledge.

He had won the eagle feather when he rescued Arcta the Giant from the spell of blindness cast on him by the Evil Wizard Malvel. Set in his shield, the feather stopped Tom from falling; instead, he floated down gently towards the Beast.

If I can land one good blow, Tom thought, *I'll defeat this dragon. I don't need to kill it. If I can force it into retreat, I can get to the Tree of Being.*

But as Tom fell, his confidence ebbed. The dragon shifted a little, waiting patiently. *Why isn't the Beast defending itself?*

When Tom was almost within range, the Beast opened its mouth, breathing a fierce gust of wind. Tom let out a cry as the blast hit him and

hurled him upwards again. He
slammed down hard onto the same
ledge he had jumped from.

Tom rolled over twice and sat up
dizzily, feeling furious and foolish all
at once. As soon as the gust of wind
died, Elenna ran over and grabbed
him by the shoulders.

"Are you all right?" she asked anxiously.

"I'm fine," Tom replied, though his side was aching where he had hit the ledge. He felt his arms and legs carefully and wiped blood away from one hand where he had scraped his skin.

But although he spoke confidently, inside he felt fierce tingles of fear running through him. *How can I fight that sort of power?* he asked himself.

"We need to think of another way to attack," Tom went on. "Whatever happens, I won't give up my Quest!"

Harsh laughter rang out from above Tom's head. "Then it will be your last," said the voice of Sanpao the Pirate King.

CHAPTER SIX

SANPAO'S CHALLENGE

Tom looked up to see the pirate ship shredding a cloud as it floated above their heads. Its red sails billowed out and its flags fluttered in the breeze. Slime dripped from its barnacle-encrusted hull.

Sanpao the Pirate King was leaning over the rail, looking down at Tom and Elenna with a mocking sneer on

his scarred face, his left eye pushed
half shut by an old wound. The
golden light from the Beast sparkled
on the darts stuck in the Pirate King's
braided, oily hair.

Tom felt a jolt of confidence as he watched the ship sink down, then rise again, swaying and turning. The helmsman, Kimal, was desperately looking for a stretch of flat ground big enough for the vessel.

"They can't land," he said to Elenna. "There are too many sharp rocks."

Elenna nodded. "Sanpao is trying to look confident," she said. "He won't want to admit to us that things aren't going his way."

"Insolent young whipper-snapper!" Sanpao laughed, "You think you're so brave, but you'll fail this time. Torno the Hurricane Dragon will blast you into dust."

Tom scrambled to his feet and pointed his sword at the pirate. "I will defeat you, whatever it takes," he promised.

Sanpao glanced over his shoulder at the helmsman. "Fly lower, Kimal!" he ordered. As the ship sank closer to Tom and Elenna, he went on, "Admit it, you are defeated. Torno has claimed the Tree of Being."

Tom cast a swift glance down to where the golden dragon was still perched, with his talons gripping the trunk of the magic tree. The Beast's gleaming gaze seemed to challenge him.

It will take more than the threats of a pirate to make me turn my back on a Beast Quest, Tom thought.

Turning to Elenna, he spoke softly into her ear. "Shoot your arrows at Torno, to get his attention."

Elenna nodded, unslinging her bow from her back and pulling an arrow from her quiver.

Torno's head turned as Elenna fitted shaft after shaft to her bow and loosed them at the Beast. They swished through the air; Torno fixed his eyes on them as they drew closer. His jaws gaped as he created a swirling gust of wind that sent the arrows spinning and flipping all the way back to Elenna, where they fell on to the ledge around her feet.

Sanpao let out a bellow of laughter. Tom looked up to see his pirate crew crowding to the ship's rail; they jeered and pointed, clearly believing that Elenna's attack had failed.

They underestimate me, Tom thought with a grin of satisfaction. Elenna ignored the pirates as she scooped the arrows up and sent them back at Torno.

While the Beast was aiming his fierce gales at Elenna, Tom launched himself into the air again, holding up his shield so that Arcta's eagle feather would stop him from falling. As he thrust himself downwards he held out his sword, the point of the blade aimed squarely at Torno's golden neck.

"Look out!" roared Sanpao. "He's trying to trick you!"

Tom tensed his muscles, ready to drive his sword home. But before Tom could strike, Torno's head swung round, and he slashed a mighty claw through the air.

Tom dragged his shield down just in time, flinching as Torno's powerful talons raked across its surface. The

next instant, another blast of hot wind seized Tom and hurled him upwards. All the breath was knocked out of him as he thumped down on to the ledge.

Tom heard mocking laughter from Sanpao overhead. Burning with frustration, he sat up and examined his shield. Two deep claw-marks were scored across it.

Beside him, Elenna reached out and touched the claw-marks. "What?" she breathed. "Your shield has never been damaged before..."

If that had been my body, I'd have been torn in two! Tom thought, suppressing a shudder. "I know," he said. "It just shows what a powerful enemy Torno is."

Before Tom could think what to do next, a shadow fell over him.

"Elenna! Be careful!" he yelled, looking up and seeing Sanpao aiming down the sight of his crossbow, a wicked grin on his face. He had brought the ship lower, to give himself the chance of a better shot.

"Die, pesky Avantians!" the Pirate King cried, releasing a bolt.

Tom threw himself flat, and heard it whizz over his head as Elenna darted behind the nearest boulder. Tom was about to scramble over to her when he heard a loud rumbling. The mountain ledge beneath his body shook. Tom peered over the edge to see that Torno was on the move. The Beast had left the tree and was clawing his way towards Tom, ripping holes in the rocks as he moved.

Time's running out!

As another crossbow bolt hit the

ground beside him, Tom rolled into
the shelter of the boulder beside
Elenna. She loosed another arrow
at the pirate ship, the point burying
itself in the rail, close enough to
make Sanpao jump back.

"If only there was a way to distract the pirates!" she muttered.

Then an idea struck Tom. *Maybe there is…*

Turning his shield so that the outside faced him, Tom touched the eagle feather to summon his friend, Arcta the Mountain Giant.

"I wish I had my red jewel," he whispered to Elenna. "That way I could tell Arcta what I need him to do."

He had hardly finished speaking when he heard another rumbling sound. It was distant at first, then grew louder and louder, as if thunder was rolling out overhead. Steady footsteps, like short earthquakes, shook the rocks.

"It's Arcta!" Elenna cried. "He's here!"

CHAPTER SEVEN

ARCTA TO THE RESCUE

"The Beast! It's the Beast!"

Tom peered out from behind the rock to see three of Sanpao's pirates rush to the rail of the ship where the Pirate King stood. Their faces were white with terror as they babbled out warnings.

"Quick, turn about, King Sanpao!"

"We told you a monster lurked in the mountains!"

75

"The Beast will kill us all!"

Tom smiled grimly as he recognised the pirate scouts who had tracked them to their cave the night before.

"Sanpao must have picked them up earlier," he said.

"And they know all about Arcta!" Elenna added with a grin.

Sanpao let out a roar of fury. Spinning round, he knocked all three of the pirates to the deck. "Lily-livered cowards!" he shouted. "This is what you get for failing in the mission I gave you!"

Sanpao aimed a heavy kick at the nearest pirate, and turned back to grip the ship's rail. Tom grinned with satisfaction to see the Pirate King staring around to see where the noise was coming from.

This is something he didn't expect!

Tom ventured out from the shelter of the rock. The rumbling and shaking continued, but he couldn't see Arcta. Instead, a golden glow spilt over the ledge, and Torno's great shining head rose up from below. There was hardly a spear's length between them. The dragon's jaws stretched wide, his long fangs gleaming. His eyes glowed with malice as he spotted Tom and let out a long, threatening snarl.

Tom raisied his sword and shield to defend himself.

Suddenly Torno's head whipped to the right and his snarl rose to a bellow of defiance as Arcta emerged among the mountain peaks. His head towered above the rocks, as he plunged forward, his massive hands reaching out to grab Torno. His fingers, tipped with yellow claws, were hooked ready to close around the evil Beast's neck.

The fearsome dragon spread his wings and rose into the air, mounting high above Arcta. Then he swooped on the good Beast in a golden blur, talons stretched out to tear at the Mountain Giant's face.

Arcta aimed a punched at him. Torno's sleek body spun as he veered sharply away, but the edge of one wing clipped Arcta's pumping fist and the Hurricane Dragon was sent spinning. He righted himself with a wide turn in the sky and shot forward for another attack.

Tom and Elenna stood side by side on the ledge, their gaze fixed on the battle. Tom's heart pounded as he watched the two Beasts locked in combat. He gasped when he saw Torno's claws sink into Arcta's forearm, blood gushing out and staining Arcta's brown fur.

"No!" Tom cried. With a pained growl, the good Beast swatted Torno away, but the dragon simply flipped over and batted the giant about the face with his wings.

Tom stifled a cry as Arcta fell back heavily among the rocks. He wanted to look away. Had he summoned his great friend to his death?

"Tear him to pieces!" Sanpao yelled, shaking his fist from where he watched in the safety of his ship. "Pull out his guts and feed them to the birds!"

Arcta bellowed a deep-throated roar of rage as he made a grab for Torno.

"That's it!" Tom called out. "Fight back, Arcta!"

Arcta managed to seize Torno's neck and hurled him off into the sky. Torno kept his balance, but instead of returning for another assault, he flew

away, heading further into the
mountains, with Arcta pounding
after him. Both Beasts disappeared
among the peaks, and gradually the
sound of Arcta's trampling footsteps
died away.

Tom felt Elenna clutch at him excitedly. "Arcta won!" she said. "He chased Torno off!"

"And now the way is clear," Tom added, his heart soaring as he scented victory. "I can get to the Tree of Being."

"But we still have to deal with Sanpao," said Elenna, pointing down from the ledge where they stood.

Tom looked down from the ledge to see that Sanpao's ship was floating in the air on a level with the Tree of Being. Pirates were lined up along the rail, ropes and grappling irons in their hands.

"Throw them at the roots!" Sanpao ordered. "We'll rip the Tree right out of the mountain."

Tom exchanged a horrified glance with Elenna. He had assumed that if

Sanpao couldn't land his ship, he couldn't get near the Tree. He hadn't considered that they might try uprooting it in mid-air.

"We've got to do something!" Elenna muttered.

What can I do? Tom wondered desperately. *I can't sprout wings!*

He had only moments to act. If Sanpao took the Tree of Being, then Avantia – and any other kingdom the Pirate King desired – would lie helpless before him.

"I will not let this happen!" Tom yelled. "Elenna, cover me!"

Raising his shield and calling on the power of the eagle feather once more, Tom jumped off the ledge and swooped towards the Tree of Being.

CHAPTER EIGHT

ABOARD THE PIRATE SHIP

Grappling irons thrust out from the pirate ship, biting deep into the trunk and branches of the Tree of Being. Tom landed lightly on his feet on one of the ropes that linked the ship to the Tree.

"Hey! Look at that!" one of the pirates cried out.

"Shoot him down!" Sanpao snarled,

waving his cutlass to beckon his crew
to the ship's rail. "I want his bones
ground up and scattered to the winds!"

Spreading his arms for balance and
trying not to look down, Tom walked
along the rope, heading for Sanpao's
ship.

Pirates bustled across the deck, and
a crossbowman took aim at Tom. He

stretched back the mechanism. "We don't take stowaways," he sneered.

As he was about to shoot, an arrow struck his arm. The pirate dropped his crossbow with a yelp of pain.

Tom turned to see Elenna holding her bow and grinning in triumph.

"Thanks!" Tom shouted.

"Keep shooting!" Sanpao yelled. "Strike him down!"

His pirates stayed back from the rail, all eyeing Elenna in fear.

Tom had almost reached the ship. *Just one more step...*

Sanpao roared in fury as Tom leaped over the gunwale and onto the deck.

"Chop him up for fish-bait!" yelled the Pirate King.

The pirates rushed at Tom, cutlasses drawn. Tom swirled his sword in rapid, arcing movements to keep them at bay. None of them dared venture within reach of the flashing blade. A huge, muscular pirate hoisted a barrel over his head with a grunt and flung it. Tom only just managed to duck and the barrel flew over his head, bounced off the deck and crashed into the ship's rail.

Another pirate charged, slashing his cutlass at Tom's knees. Tom hopped over the whirling blade and shoved the pirate with his shield. He leaped into the rigging and swung by one hand from a spar that held the sails, kicking out at the pirates as they tried to grab him.

"Useless fools!" Sanpao snarled at his men, stepping forward and drawing his jagged blade. "Stand aside! I'll be the one to bring this

land-lubber down, once and for all."
Looking up at Tom, he added, "Do
you dare fight me?"

"Gladly," Tom replied.

Letting go of the spar, he landed
lightly on the deck as the rest of the
pirates gathered in a circle around
Tom and the Pirate King. They
stamped their feet on the deck in
a fierce rhythm, chanting, "San-pao!
San-pao! San-pao!"

"Is that supposed to frighten me?"
said Tom. "Because it's not working!"

Sanpao drew his lips back in
a bloodthirsty grin. "Oh, you think
you're so brave! But you'll be
screaming for your mother by the
time I've finished with you." Sanpao
laughed. "Not that she'll be able to
hear you. Not when she's so very
far away."

Tom yelled in anger as he bounded forward, sweeping his sword round to aim a stab at the Pirate King's heart. Sanpao brought up his own blade, and the two weapons clashed together.

Instantly Tom leapt to one side, swiping his sword at Sanpao's neck, forcing him to take a backwards step.

Sanpao looked Tom up and down, his grin fading fast.

You thought I was an inexperienced boy, Tom said to himself. *Now you can see I'm not so easily dealt with.*

The Pirate King lunged forwards, attacking Tom with a rapid flurry of stabs, trying to drive him back into the circle of pirates. Tom dodged aside and forced Sanpao to face him. Their weapons clanged and clashed together as Tom hacked at Sanpao's cutlass, trying to break the Pirate King's guard. He could hear gasps from the surrounding pirates – they sensed that Sanpao was losing the fight.

"Come on, Tom!" Elenna shouted from the ledge. "You've got him on the run!"

Sanpao stepped back, his scarred face twisting in alarm. He was breathing harder.

"Tired, are you?" Tom taunted him.

Sanpao growled. "Never! I'll use your skin for sail-cloth first!"

Tom jabbed, and Sanpao stumbled back a step, blocking clumsily. Tom advanced once more, pushing the Pirate King's blade aside. Sanpao cried out as he tripped over a coil of rope and his dropped cutlass hit the deck just before he did.

Tom raised his sword to strike the blow that would finish the fight. Sanpao's eyes widened in fear and astonishment. "Curse you, boy!" he snarled.

Something struck Tom on the ankle. He fell forwards, sprawling on to the deck. In a flash, Sanpao was

towering over him, one foot pinning
Tom's sword arm, while he aimed the
point of his cutlass at Tom's throat.

The pirates' chanting broke up into
cheers and roars of laughter. Furious,
Tom realised that one of them must
have stuck out a foot to trip him.

"Not so brave now, are you?"
Sanpao sneered. "Surrender!"

Tom shook his head. "Not while there's blood in my veins!"

He felt fear welling up inside him. With Sanpao's foot on his arm, he couldn't use his sword, and his only other weapon was the trident he had won from Hecton. But that was tightly fastened in his belt, and it was an unfamiliar weapon that he would have to wield with his left hand.

Fumbling for the trident, Tom managed to wrench it free. Sanpao let out a mocking laugh and drew back his cutlass to slash it down over Tom's throat. But before he could strike, the ship lurched, sending the pirates staggering about the deck. Their cheers and laughter became cries of terror.

The weight of Sanpao's foot on Tom's arm relaxed just enough for Tom to wriggle free. With his sword in one hand and the trident in the other he sprang to his feet, staring around to find out what had caused the ship's sudden movement. A grin spread over his face. "I might have known it!" he cried.

Elenna was shooting her arrows at the ropes hooked into the Tree of Being. Several of them already hung loose. As Tom watched, the strands of another rope split apart and Sanpao's ship gave another violent shift as it separated from the mountain face. "More ropes!" roared the Pirate King. "And kill that wretched girl!"

CHAPTER NINE

BATTLE WITH THE BEAST

Tom sheathed his sword and scrambled on to the rail of the ship, then launched himself at the cliff. He held the trident out in front of him and drove the prongs into a crack to pin himself to the rock face.

Above his head, Elenna fired two arrows at the ship's mainsail, tearing a rope in the rigging. As the sail folded over at one corner, the prow dipped and the stern swung sideways with a creak of timbers. Pirates lost their balance and slid across the deck, yelling out to each other with panicked cries. The ship sank lower as Kimal the helmsman struggled against the wheel to control it.

"Well done!" Tom called to his friend. "That will keep them busy!"

Looking over his shoulder, Tom saw Sanpao grasp the rail to haul himself up at the prow. "It will take more than a few arrows to defeat the Pirates of Makai!" he bellowed, shaking his fist.

As Tom clung to the trident he saw the Pirate King stumble across the deck to his sail, the mast of which was made from wood stolen from the Tree of Being. He grabbed hold of it and looked to the sky.

"Return!" Sanpao bellowed. "Kill this pesky boy!"

Out of the corner of his eye, Tom spotted a golden glint in the air above the mountain peaks. The gleam grew larger and Tom realised it was Torno. His heart lurched. *That's how Sanpao controls the Beasts*, he realised. *The magic he has stolen from the Tree of Being gives him this power. He's my most dangerous enemy yet.*

Then Tom's heart sank. *Where is Arcta?* he wondered. The Hurricane Dragon flew through the air to hover once more above the Tree of Being.

"Ha!" shouted Sanpao. "My pet has returned!"

Tom's hope flared when he saw Arcta's head rise up from behind the shoulder of the mountain. He leaped

nimbly from rock to rock until he
stood below Torno at the bottom of
the precipice.

Tom's stomach churned as he
realised that Arcta was getting the
worst of the fight. Arcta grabbed for
the dragon, but Torno hovered

higher, blasting the giant with air
that flattened his fur. Arcta was
forced to stoop, one arm held across
his face, as he struggled to get closer
to his enemy.

"Fight back, Arcta!" Tom called.
"You can do it!"

The Mountain Giant heard his
encouragement. He reached for
a handhold and tried to drag himself
further up, towards where the Tree
of Being gripped the rockface. His
free hand broke from the path of the
hurricane and swatted blindly at the
pirate ship. The force of the blow
smashed the hull and sent the boat
into a spiral.

Tom heard yells of terror from the
pirates on the deck as the vessel spun
helplessly downwards into the abyss.
He caught a glimpse of Sanpao

looking up, his face fixed in a snarl of rage. Then the shape of the falling ship dwindled and plunged beneath a layer of cloud.

The Pirates of Makai were gone.

"I hope that's the last we see of them!" Tom muttered, though he knew that he and Sanpao were destined to face each other again.

Tom dug the toes of his boots and

his fingers into the rock face as he used the trident to climb towards the Tree of Being. He scrambled on to its trunk. Now that he was so close to it, he could see clearly how magnificent it was, and he laid a hand against the bark, feeling the magic within. Once Tom was safely on the magical Tree, the trident in his hand crumbled to ash, which drifted away on the light mountain breeze. Like all the other tokens Tom had won on this Quest, he could use it only once before it disappeared forever.

Looking up again, Tom saw Torno swooping on Arcta and snapping his fangs at the Good Beast's face. Arcta was forced back against the mountainside.

The Tree of Being lurched and quivered, almost throwing Tom off.

With mounting terror, he saw the roots tearing free of the rocks. He clung desperately to the trunk.

"Hold on, Tom!" shouted Elenna. "I'm coming!"

Tom gazed up through the branches to see his friend beginning to pick her way down the cliff face towards him.

"No! Stay back!" he yelled, as he heard the Tree creak. "Torno's weight has weakened the Tree. Your weight might be too much. If the Tree is destroyed, our Quest is over, and you know what that means..."

Elenna's face paled as she grew still. "We'll never find Silver and Freya," she answered.

Tom looked down in horror at Arcta, his faithful friend, slumped and defeated among the rocks. Torno loomed over him once more, as if ready to strike – but then, the Beast's gaze turned to Tom. He floated through the air with deadly menace in his eyes. Tom knew that another of the fearsome Beast's hurricanes was coming, and he braced himself to meet it, gripping the branches of the Tree as tight as he could.

Torno spun his sleek body in tight circles, creating a fierce blast of wind. Tom dug his fingers into the bark of the Tree, but his efforts to cling on were useless. The rough bark scraped across his palms as the wind ripped him from the tree and sent him tumbling. The sky and the mountain whirled around Tom as he was tossed this way and that on the violent gusts. He struggled to hold up his shield to use the power of the eagle feather, but it made no difference.

He's not trying to kill me…he's just playing with me!

Torno's gale flung Tom closer to the cliff face. Desperately Tom reached out with his sword and drove the blade into a crack in the rock. He clung to the hilt with every scrap of his strength. The wind blew him out sideways, but he refused to let go.

The wind died. Tom shook his head clear and managed to wedge the toes of his boots into a crack in the rock to balance himself. Torno prowled on the air towards him, snarling hungrily. Gasping with relief, Tom let go of his sword and managed to find footholds and handholds in Torno's clawprints. He felt the stone crumble, and saw a crack opening up in the mountainside, the rocks pushed aside by a root from the Tree of Being. He reached a narrow ledge. *My only hope is to outwit the Beast*, he thought. *Maybe I can use his claw prints against him.*

Grabbing his sword out of the crack, Tom waved it teasingly at the Hurricane Dragon. "Come on!" he shouted. "Come and get me!"

CHAPTER TEN

VICTORY OR DEFEAT?

Torno slammed his claws into the
rock face and bounded towards Tom.
Debris pattered down the slope and
spilled off the rocks to the unseen
ground below.

Tom slung his shield over his
forearm and gripped it tightly with
the same hand. In the other, he held
his sword at the ready. His head

swam as he glanced down into the depths, and he felt a surge of nausea.

His breath came faster with a mixture of excitement and fear. *One false step and I'll fall to my death.*

He caught a glimpse of Elenna leaning over the ledge above, her eyes wide and her bow poised. But there was no time to explain to her what he was trying to do.

"Get back!" he called. "Find something to hang on to!"

Torno paced closer and closer, his eyes glittering with the thrill of closing in on his prey. His steps became heavier, punching even deeper holes into the mountain; and showering chunks of rock into the depths.

"Come on..." Tom muttered. "Just two more steps...one more..."

Torno reached his earlier claw-mark, the one to which Tom was clinging. Tom braced himself, close enough now to stretch out and touch the Beast.

Torno extended one limb, his talons stretched out to tear Tom to pieces. But the mountain was weakened by the claw-marks that riddled the rocks. With a shuddering crunch, the cliff face crumbled away under the weight of Torno's massive body.

Tom let out a startled cry as the rock he was holding gave way. He grabbed vainly at the cliff face, then he was tumbling down in the midst of a rain of stones, with Torno twisting and turning wildly beside him.

Torno righted himself. Before the dragon could fly out of reach, Tom brought his sword down with a fierce

hacking motion. It cut through one
of Torno's frilled wings, slicing it
in half.

The dragon let out a shrill cry of
pain and fury and swiped at Tom
with outstretched claws, but he was
too far away. His one uninjured wing

couldn't support him as he tumbled through the air. Tom watched as the Beast went spinning and crashing to his doom in a growing avalanche of rocks and boulders.

But Tom was still plummeting through the air. As he turned, his shield slid down his arm. Tom made a grab for it, missed, and stared in horror as it fell away from him towards the ground.

Is this the last of my Beast Quests? Tom asked himself. *Am I going to—?*

"Oof!"

The breath was knocked out of Tom as he landed on what felt like hard ground. But it wasn't hard enough to crush the life out of him. Dazed, he stretched out one hand, and felt that he was lying on a leathery surface, edged with fur. He heard a long

grumble of satisfaction high above
his head.

Tom looked up to see that he had
been caught in the mighty hand of
Arcta. The Good Beast smiled down
at Tom as he held him safe. The blaze
of battle had faded from his brown
eyes; now they were warm and kind.
His face was covered with scrapes
and bruises, but to Tom's relief he
didn't seem to have been badly hurt
in the fight with Torno.

Tom heard Elenna crying out,
"You're all right!" Her voice was filled
with joy.

As Arcta placed Tom gently on
a mountain path, Tom spotted his
friend running down to meet him.
She skidded to a halt beside him,
smiling broadly.

"Thank you, Arcta," Tom said,

gazing up into the giant's face. "And thank you, too, Elenna," he added. "Without both of you, our Quest would be finished."

Arcta slowly bowed his huge head.

"Look, Tom, there's your shield," Elenna said, pointing further down the mountainside.

Tom noticed that his shield was hanging just below, dangling by its strap from a jutting spur of rock. Lying flat on the path, he reached down the cliff and tried to grab it. But it was just out of reach.

Arcta's huge arm extended past him. Sliding the shield's strap on to the jagged nail of his little finger, he lifted it up and held it out to Tom.

"I thought I'd lost it forever," Tom said as he slung the shield over his arm again, "and all the tokens that

I won from Avantia's good Beasts."

For a moment Arcta remained on his knees, staring down the mountainside. Tom followed his gaze, to the debris where Torno had disappeared. The Beast's body lay somewhere under all that rubble, never to rise again.

At last the giant heaved a long sigh and rose to his feet.

"Farewell, Arcta," Tom said. "I hope we meet again one day."

Arcta nodded and turned away, striding off along the mountain path. Tom watched his loyal friend disappear into the mountain mists. As he turned to Elenna, he saw her waving, but then her eyes widened. "What's that?" she asked, pointing down into the abyss.

Tom saw a faint speck of gold in the

air, floating up from the jumble of rocks below. He grew tense at the sight, gripping his sword hilt firmly.

"Is Torno coming back?" he asked.

But as the gleaming speck drew closer, Tom saw that it was a lone dragon scale, drifting through the air until it spiralled into Tom's outstretched hand.

"The next token!" Tom exclaimed.

"And now we can go and get the Tree of Being," Elenna added.

Tom had almost forgotten about the Tree. Looking up, he saw it was still hanging from the cliff face, high above them now. It seemed to be growing taller, its branches swelling and stretching out, covered with lush leaves.

"It looks bigger than ever," Tom said. Then he realised that the Tree's roots were straining under its weight, and the rock where they clung was beginning to crumble. "No!" he gasped. "It's getting heavier...it's going to fall!"

He began racing up the mountain path, with Elenna hard on his heels. But they were nowhere near the Tree when a loud tearing sound split the air. The Tree of Being leaned and its roots ripped out of the cliff face. The mighty trunk tipped over and the Tree tumbled down the mountainside, towards the valley where Torno lay dead and buried.

Tom and Elenna watched in horror, utterly helpless.

But before the Tree of Being hit the bottom of the cliff, green lightning cracked through the air, enveloping the tree. Tom cried out as it vanished.

"It's gone!" Elenna exclaimed.

Tom sank down on the rocky ledge, eyes fixed on the spot where the Tree of Being had been only moments before.

Has it gone for good? he wondered. *Have I failed in my Beast Quest?*

"Without the Tree, Freya and Silver are lost forever," he muttered.

Elenna sat beside him and placed a hand on his shoulder. "The Tree has always come back before," she said. "Maybe..."

She trailed off, and Tom sensed she didn't believe her own words. Every other time the Tree had vanished, its roots had sucked it back into the ground. It didn't disappear in a flash of green lightning.

He drew a deep breath, and stood up. "I won't give in," he said. "We've shown Sanpao we can face his pirates and win." He held out a hand to Elenna, who took it and rose to her feet. "Come on, let's find Storm and Blizzard."

Together, they marched down the mountainside with the sun at their backs. Their Beast Quest was not over.

While there's blood in my veins, Tom vowed, *I'll go on searching for the Tree of Being. One day, I will bring Silver and Freya back to Avantia.*

Join Tom on the next stage
of the Beast Quest where
he will battle

Kronus
THE CLAWED
MENACE

Win an exclusive
Beast Quest T-shirt and goody bag!

Tom has battled many fearsome Beasts and we want to know which one is your favourite! Send us a drawing or painting of your favourite Beast and tell us in 30 words why you think it's the best.

Each month we will select **three** winners to receive a Beast Quest T-shirt and goody bag!

Send your entry on a postcard to
BEAST QUEST COMPETITION
Orchard Books, 338 Euston Road, London NW1 3BH.

Australian readers should email:
childrens.books@hachette.com.au

New Zealand readers should write to:
Beast Quest Competition, 4 Whetu Place, Mairangi Bay, Auckland NZ, or email: childrensbooks@hachette.co.nz

**Don't forget to include your name and address.
Only one entry per child.**

Good luck!

Join the Quest,
Join the Tribe

www.beastquest.co.uk

Have you checked out the Beast Quest website?
It's the place to go for games, downloads, activities,
sneak previews and lots of fun!

You can read all about your favourite Beasts, down-
load free screensavers and desktop wallpapers for
your computer, and even challenge your friends
to a Beast Tournament.

Sign up to the newsletter at www.beastquest.co.uk
to receive exclusive extra content and the oppor-
tunity to enter special members-only competitions.
We'll send you up-to-date info on all the Beast
Quest books, including the next exciting series
which features six brand-new Beasts!

Get 30% off all Beast Quest Books at www.beastquest.co.uk
Enter the code BEAST at the checkout.

All books priced at £4.99,
special bumper editions
priced at £5.99.

Orchard Books are available from all good bookshops, or can
be ordered from our website: www.orchardbooks.co.uk,
or telephone 01235 827702, or fax 01235 8227703.

Series 8: THE PIRATE KING
COLLECT THEM ALL!

Sanpao the Pirate King wants to steal the sacred Tree
of Being. Can Tom scupper his plans?

BALISK
THE WATER SNAKE

978 1 40831 310 7

KORON
JAWS OF DEATH

978 1 40831 311 4

HECTON
THE BODY SNATCHER

978 1 40831 312 1

TORNO
THE HURRICANE DRAGON

978 1 40831 313 8

KRONUS
THE CLAWED MENACE

978 1 40831 314 5

BLOODBOAR
THE BURIED DOOM

978 1 40831 315 2

Series 9: The Warlock's Staff
Out September 2011

Meet six terrifying new Beasts!

Ursus the Clawed Roar
Minos the Demon Bull
Koraka the Winged Assassin
Silver the Wild Terror
Spikefin the Water King
Torpix the Twisting Serpent

Watch out for the next Special Bumper Edition
OUT OCT 2011!

The Chronicles of Avantia

FROM THE DARK, A HERO ARISES...

Dare to enter the kingdom of Avantia.

A new evil arises in Avantia. Lord Derthsin has ordered his armies into the four corners of Avantia. If the four Beasts of Avantia can find their Chosen Riders they might have the strength to challenge Derthsin. But if they fail, the land of Avantia will be lost forever...

FIRST HERO, CHASING EVIL AND CALL TO WAR, OUT NOW!

Fire and Fury out July 2011

www.chroniclesofavantia.com